The Prisoner

Stories linking with the History
National Curriculum Key Stage 2

First published in 1998 by Franklin Watts
338 Euston Road, London NW1 3BH

Franklin Watts Australia
Level 17/207 Kent Street, Sydney NSW 2000

This edition published 2002
Text © Penny McKinlay 1998

Editor: Kyla Barber
Designer: Jason Anscomb
Consultant: Dr Anne Millard

A CIP catalogue record for this book
is available from the British Library

ISBN 978 0 7496 4598 4

Dewey Classification 941.084

Printed in Great Britain

Franklin Watts is a division of Hachette Children's Books,
an Hachette Livre UK company.
www.hachettelivre.co.uk

The Prisoner

by
Penny McKinlay

Illustrations by Greg Gormley

FRANKLIN WATTS
LONDON•SYDNEY

1

The Enemy Surrenders

"Rat-tat-tat-tat-tat!" The sound of
machine-gun fire shattered the dreamy
September warmth of the wheat-field.
"Come out, now, with your hands up!"
shouted Bob. "I've got you covered!"

He waved his wooden stick

threateningly at the
haystack. He knew Jack
was hiding behind it.

"Rat-tat-
tat-tat!" he
screamed again.
"You're dead
now, Jack!
I've won!"

Silence.
Nothing moved. Then:
"STOP THIS, STOP, STOP!"

The dark body of a man hurled itself
from the top of the haystack and pinned Bob

to the ground. Terrified,
Bob screamed to Jack
for help. The stranger
pushed his face close to
his, spitting out strange
words. It was a twisted,

wild face, streaked with tears. Bob cried
out in pain as the man crushed him
against the sharp stubble
of the cut wheat.

Jack jumped
on to the man's
back, trying to pull
him off Bob. "Get
off, get off, you're
hurting him!"

The
man quite
suddenly let
go of Bob and sank back on his knees,
sobbing. Bob scrambled to his feet and
he and Jack stood watching, bewildered.
They had never seen a man cry before.
He wasn't so frightening now.

"I sorry, sorry." They were the first
words Bob could understand. "Is bad

game you play with guns! You not understand."

"He's one of those Italian prisoners," whispered Jack. "From the prisoner of war camp. He's working for my dad on the farm, getting the harvest in."

Bob stared, backed away. He shivered. It was as if Jack had just told him the man was the devil.

So this was the enemy, one of the men Dad had been fighting until he was taken prisoner and locked up in a prison camp.

Now Dad couldn't come home until the end of the war.

Bob couldn't remember when there hadn't been a war on. Five years, his mum said, but that was half Bob's life. This war that made his mum so sad and tired-looking. This war that meant nothing but horrible food. This war that meant hardly any sweets. This war that had taken his dad away. He didn't really believe the war would ever end, but he didn't say that to his mum. He didn't want to upset her.

He looked back at the man. He was quieter now, staring at them. There was something about his eyes that bothered Bob. Then he remembered when he and his dad had found a fox cowering exhausted in the lane. Bob had

never forgotten the animal's eyes, pleading for help. Moments later the hunters and the fox-hounds swept round the corner and the fox was killed.

Bob suddenly realised that this man,

this enemy, was scared of them.

"I'm going to tell my dad." Jack was the first to speak. "You'll be punished, they won't let you out of the camp again."

"Please, no tell!" cried the man. He struggled to find the right English words to explain. "Bang! Bang! The shooting, for you is a game. For me, is real. My friends, they all died. I cannot forget."

Just then came a shout.

"Mario, Mario!" It was Jack's dad. Bob called him Uncle Leonard, but he wasn't a real uncle. Like their mums and dads, Jack and Bob had grown up together in the village. But when the war came Bob's dad had to go away to fight. Now Bob secretly felt jealous of Jack because his dad didn't have to go to war. He was a farmer  and he was needed to stay at home and grow food for everyone, 'Digging for Victory!' like it said on all the posters.

When the Italian heard Uncle Leonard calling, he jumped up and ran back to join the other men hard at work harvesting. He shouted back over his shoulder, "Please, no tell. I sorry."

The two friends picked up their sticks

and walked silently back towards the farm. Neither of them felt like shooting each other any more.

"Don't tell, Jack," Bob said suddenly.

"Why not?" argued Jack. "He hurt you." Bob stopped. He didn't know why. He kept seeing that fox, those eyes.

"I just feel sorry for him, I suppose." Jack stared at him.

"Sorry for an Italian!" he exploded. "They're the enemy. What if your dad heard you saying that?" Bob felt tears pricking behind his eyes. He didn't want Jack to see, so he broke into a run.

"I've got to get home for my tea," he shouted back. "I'll see you tomorrow!" And he took off across the fields, running away from all these questions with no answers.

2
Making Do

Back home, Bob burst into the kitchen to be greeted by the usual smell of cabbage and the unusual sight of a girl standing on a chair, dipping a rag into a jug of brown stuff and rubbing it on her legs.

"What on earth are you doing, Nell?"

"Painting my legs with gravy browning," said Nell, as if it was the most normal thing in the world. Nell was from London, but she was staying with them because she was working in the Land Army, helping on the farm while the men were away in the real army.

"All the girls do it, it makes you look like you've got stockings on. And since there isn't a pair of stockings to be had for love nor money out here in the wilderness, this is the best I can do – I'm going to that dance in the village tonight. Now come here and help. Can you draw in a straight line?"

"What on earth are you doing, Bob?"

cried Mum when she walked into the kitchen. Bob was concentrating on drawing a perfect straight line down the back of Nell's legs. His hand slipped.

"He's drawing the seams in for my stockings, Mrs Gander," said Nell. "Now look, Bob, you'll have to do that bit again."

Mum stared, then laughed. "Now I've seen it all! That's real 'make do and mend', that is! You're right though, Nell, I don't remember the last time I had a pair of stockings." Mum was always talking about 'make do and mend', ideas she got from the wireless and women's magazines about making old things last longer, now new clothes were rationed and hard to get. Bob hadn't had any new clothes for ages, it was all cut-down stuff of his dad's. Not that it bothered him, but he knew that Mum minded not having anything new. He remembered once they had gone to the pictures in town for his birthday. The film was full of ladies dancing in pretty dresses and when they came out he could see tears in her eyes.

"I know it's a wicked thing to cry over when people are dying every day," she sniffed. "But, Bob, I'd give anything to go out dancing with

16

your dad again in a dress like that."

Bob looked at her smiling now. Mum was a lot happier since Nell had come to live with them. Nell made them laugh with her stories about working on the farm.

"What's for supper, Mum?" he asked, not very hopefully.

"Cabbage pie," replied Mum. "With –"

"Plenty of potatoes!" interrupted Nell and Bob together. "Not again!"

Mum looked upset.

"That's all there is," she apologised.

"I queued up for ages at the butcher but there was nothing left. He's promised us something for tomorrow."

"Don't worry, Mum," said Bob quickly. Why couldn't they put cabbage on the ration instead of sweets? He thought how to cheer Mum up. "Nell, tell us about the tomatoes again!"

Nell groaned. "Not that old one!" But as they sat down to eat she told Bob's favourite story again, about the day she started in the Land Army. "I'd never been near a farm in my life! Never been out of London, in fact," she began. "I only went for the Land Army because I liked the

uniform! Anyway,
first day, your
Uncle Leonard, he
takes me over to
the tomatoes.
'Here you are,
love,' he says.
'Start with
something easy.
You can shoot
the tomatoes.'

And I say, 'But I haven't got
a gun!' I didn't realise he just meant take the
new shoots off the plants to stop them
growing too fast – I didn't have a clue!"

Laughing took Bob's mind off the
cabbage pie. It also took his mind off the
Italian prisoner, but not for long. He tried to
push the thoughts away all evening, scared to
tell Mum. How would she feel about him

talking to the enemy?

"You're very quiet, love," she said that night as she tucked him into bed. "Everything all right?"

"Yes, Mum, fine."

But in the darkness his old nightmare came back. It was always the same, his dad being beaten while he stood watching, frozen to the spot. Only this time he could see the face of the man hurting his dad. It was the Italian prisoner.

"Stop it, stop it!" he shouted, and woke himself up. Mum came running in. "What is it, Bob?" And then it

all came tumbling out while Mum hugged
him safe against the rough
wool of Dad's old
overcoat that she used
as a dressing-gown.
He was a little boy
again. He told her
all about the
Italian, and she
went very quiet.

"Are you cross
with me, Mum?"
asked Bob.

"No, of
course not, Bob."
But she looked shocked.

"Trouble is, I felt sorry for him and
Jack said Dad would be angry if he knew."

Mum was silent. Her face flickered
with feelings.

"Well, Dad's a prisoner, too, Bob, so perhaps he would understand how the Italian feels. He's just another human being, after all. And we aren't even at war with Italy any more. They're on our side now." Finally, as if she had suddenly found the right answer, she said, "Anyway, I'd like to think, wherever Dad is, that someone's being kind to him. So I think we should be kind to the Italian." Bob smiled at her, relieved. "Now, what about a bit of a snack? I've made a cake with a real egg Jack's mum gave me. Come on."

Downstairs they sat together with big cups of tea and the delicious cake, not made with the usual carrots or potato.

Bob snuggled close inside Dad's overcoat. It was full of his dad's smell, and he suddenly missed him terribly. The sobs rose up from his heart and he couldn't keep them down. Mum wrapped the coat round him and held him tight until he could speak.

"This war's never going to end, is it, Mum? Tell me the truth."

Mum stared at him.

"Oh, Bob, it is going to end. We're beating the Germans everywhere now." She paused. "I suppose for you it seems to have gone on for ever."

Bob nodded miserably.

"Look," said Mum. She pulled the map of Europe out of the drawer. Then

she pinned it up on the wall.

"I put this away when the war was going so badly. Let's put it back up, and after

24

we've listened to the news on the wireless every day we'll move the little flags for each army. Then you'll see, we are winning now. And how about this!" Mum threw open the

thick black curtains that stopped the lights showing to the enemy aircraft so they couldn't drop bombs on them.

"Mum!" cried Bob, terrified. "What about the blackout! You'll get into trouble!"

"No, I won't," replied Mum. "Come and see!"

Bob went over to the window. The village street, pitch black at night throughout the war, was lit up like fairyland. "The street lights are back on, Bob," said Mum, smiling. "It's the beginning of the end."

26

3
"Ciao!"

Bob didn't see the Italian again for a
while, until one cold Saturday morning in
the autumn Mum announced they had to
help Uncle Leonard on the farm.

"Oh, Mum!" groaned Bob. He'd
planned to play football as usual.

"Bob!" Mum was really angry. "Everyone has to do their bit to help, that's what's got us through this war!"

And so it was that Bob ended up in a field digging up turnips next to the Italian. He kept his head down, embarrassed.

"Ciao!" the Italian said suddenly.

"Where?" said Bob, startled. He looked round. He thought he said 'cow'. The Italian laughed. It was a nice laugh.

"Not cow – 'ciao!'" he repeated. "In my country, means 'hello'."

He stretched out his hand, and Bob

---

* 'Ciao' is Italian for 'hello' - say it 'chow'

shook it politely. The skin was rough and cracked.

"You need gloves," said Bob.

"Yes. England is too cold. Not like Italy!" His English had got better. "How old are you?"

"Ten," said Bob.

"My little brother, Roberto, he is ten, like you," said the Italian.

"That's my name, Robert," said Bob, surprised.

"I am Mario," said the Italian. Then he added quietly, "Roberto is like you, he loves football. I miss him, and my mother."

Bob plucked up courage to ask a question. "Where do you live, in England I mean? Are you locked up in prison?"

"No, we live in a big camp. Is not bad, better than when we were fighting. Since Italy stop fighting with Germans and join British side, some Italians, they leave camp and live on farms. Is better, I think. More like home."

They talked all afternoon. Mario seemed glad to talk about his family. Bob watched sadly in the cold dusk as Mario climbed into the back of the lorry to go back to the prison camp.

He and Jack went into the warm farm kitchen. Mum and Auntie May had made a big tea and Uncle Leonard was already tucking in.

"Auntie May, why can't Mario live here instead of at the camp?" Bob suddenly burst out. "He misses his family – he'd be much happier here!"

"Bob!" scolded his mum. "That's none of our business!"

But Bob couldn't stop.

"Please, Uncle Leonard," he begged.

"Dad's a prisoner too – it's like someone being kind to him."

Uncle Leonard looked doubtful.

"I don't know, Bob, it's a big responsibility. What if he disappears, tries to go back to Italy? I'll get the blame."

"I'll keep an eye on him," promised Bob.

"I'll think about it," was all Uncle Leonard would say.

4
The Camp

Uncle Leonard did think about it. Next Saturday he drove up to Bob's cottage in his truck. Jack was with him.

"Hop in," he said. "We're going to fetch your Italian friend."

The camp was a big field with tall

fences, topped with barbed wire. Uncle
Leonard stopped at the gate, and the guards
waved him through. While he was sorting
things out with a man in uniform, Bob and
Jack stared around. It was very bleak, with
thick mud everywhere. There were long rows
of huts and inside Bob got a glimpse of long
rows of narrow beds. No wonder Mario
missed home.

Then Mario climbed in beside them. He

was smiling, and his face looked suddenly quite different.

"Thank you," he said simply.

Mario soon settled in, in a spare room at the top of the farmhouse. Sometimes at weekends he played football with the boys, and even Jack admitted he was 'all right really'.

One morning, about six weeks before Christmas, Mum was round at the farm.

She and Auntie May had put their points together to get enough dried fruit for a proper Christmas cake. Everyone crowded round the bowl to stir the cake and make a wish. Bob wished for Dad to come home soon.

"No secret what we're all wishing for," said Auntie May. "Let's hope this is our last war-time Christmas."

Mario and Nell came in. They had been out working together.

"Come and have a wish, you two!" said Mum.

Nell smiled at Mario shyly, and they took it in turns to wish.

All afternoon delicious cake smells wafted through the open window. Later

Bob saw the cake cooling on the window-sill.

Suddenly there was a scream and a squawk, and the ginger tom-cat came tearing out as if his tail was on fire. Auntie May chased after him with the kitchen knife in her hand.

Bob and Jack went inside. There was the cake with a big hole in the middle.

"But cats don't eat cake!" said Bob.

"Tell Ginger that!" said Auntie May.

Nell and Mario rushed in. Nell gasped: "What a waste of rations!"

"No, not waste!" said Mario firmly.

He took the knife from Auntie May and cut away the edges of the hole. Then he took the pretend marzipan Mum and Auntie May had made and filled in the gap. They all watched in amazement as his fingers worked, shaping the marzipan on top of the cake into all sorts of wonderful flowers, birds and animals. By the time he had finished, the cake was a work of art.

"Why, it's lovely, Mario," said Mum.

"I love to cook," said Mario smiling. "In Italy, is my job."

Jack looked as though Mario had said he could fly.

"Men don't cook," he said bluntly.

"In my country, men cook," said Mario. And he described the food in Italy. His whole face lit up as he talked of things they had never heard of, spaghetti and pizzas and many other strange-sounding things. "One day, I will make these things for you, after the war."

5

The Runaway

The weeks before Christmas were endless
– it was a bitterly cold winter that seemed
to go on and on. At last Christmas Eve
came, as snowy as a scene on a Christmas
card. In the morning a thick envelope
arrived, with a letter each for Mum and

Bob from Dad in the prison camp. Bob liked to read Dad's letters in private, so he could hear his voice in his head. He ran down to the barn. He climbed the huge wall of straw and snuggled down.

Dad's letter was full of stuff about playing football in the prison camp, and he asked about Jack, and school. He never complained, but he sounded so sad.

"I do miss you, Bob, and your mum," he wrote. "This war seems to go on for ever. But it will end, and soon we will all be together again. I love you, son. Dad."

The sudden sound of a man weeping sent a shiver through Bob. For a moment he thought he was hearing Dad, hundreds of miles away. After the first shock Bob realised the weeping was coming from inside the barn. He peered down. In the half-light he could make out Mario, his body hunched into a ball of misery.

"Mamma!" Bob could hear him

whispering. "Mamma!" Bob did not know
what to do. Mario suddenly stood up,
dashing tears from his eyes, and
stormed out.

Bob quickly slid down the straw and
made for the door. A piece of paper was
trapped underneath. He picked it up.
It was a letter, but he couldn't read it. It
was in Italian.

Bob peered out into the snowy
farmyard, then ducked back in. Mario
was wheeling Uncle Leonard's bike out

from the shed. He had a kit bag on his back, and as Bob peeped out again, he cycled off, the wheels sliding in the slushy snow.

He was running away!

Bob stood in the doorway, horrified. He felt as frozen as Jack's snowman. He promised Uncle Leonard he'd keep an eye on Mario. Now Mario was running away and Uncle Leonard would get into trouble.

Then he saw Jack coming out of the back door, wrapped up warm with his wellies and scarf and hat.

"Jack!" he hissed. "Jack, over here!" He put his fingers to his lips. Jack trudged over and Bob pulled him quickly inside. "Mario's run away!" Bob announced. Jack's eyes went round as gobstoppers. "He must have had bad news from Italy – look!" Bob showed Jack the letter. "What shall we do?"

"Get Nell!" said Jack.

"Why Nell?" demanded Bob.

"Because they're sweet on each other, stupid. My mum said," replied Jack. "Nell will get him to come back, you'll see."

Nell was having a few days off from the farm for Christmas, so the boys struggled back down the snowy lane to Bob's house. They watched through the window until Mum left Nell alone in the kitchen. She was getting ready to go out that night, her hair tightly curled in twists of paper.

"What are you up to, you two?" she said crossly when she came to the door. "Playing German spies again?" But her face changed as they explained. "I'm coming," she said. "Wait for me in the farmyard."

When she joined them she was in her thick Land Army coat and hat and heavy boots. She shouted to Uncle Leonard: "I'm taking the tractor to check on those sheep, Len!" and then swung herself up, tiny behind the big wheel. The boys started to climb on after her. "Oh, no you don't!" she said firmly. "You've got to follow the tracks!"

Off they went along the lane, the two boys following the narrow tyre marks, wider sometimes where the bike had slipped in the snow.

"He's fallen off a few times," said Jack. "Trust an Italian not to know you can't ride a bike in the snow!"

But Mario hadn't given up. Mile after mile the strange procession crept along, and soon it started to get dark. Nell put the headlamps on, but they could hardly see the bicycle tracks.

At last they came to a crossroads. The tracks disappeared.

"He must be heading for the coast, to try and get a ship home," said Bob.

"But which way is the coast?" cried Nell.

There were no road signs – they had been taken down at the start of the war to confuse the Germans if they invaded.

"I'm hungry," said Jack. "Let's go home."

Nell got down and walked ahead, shining a torch. She wouldn't give up. Then suddenly the boys saw someone lurch out of the hedge.

"Nell!"

"Oh, Mario, we were so worried!" Nell cried as they hugged each other. "Boys!" she shouted. "He's here, we've found him."

Uncle Leonard's bike lay with a twisted wheel where Mario had hit a stone in the

snow. Together the boys loaded it into the
trailer, while Nell helped the shivering Mario
on to the tractor.

"My mother, Nell," he was saying, over
and over. "She is sick, I must go – there is
no one to look after her."

"Mario," said Nell gently. "You can't go,
you have to stay in England until the war
ends. She'll be all right, you'll see."

"And what about my dad?" piped up
Jack. "You'll get him into trouble, too!"

"Anyway, we'd miss you," said Bob.

"Besides," said Nell. "You said you'd take me to the Christmas Eve dance tonight." She pulled her Land Army hat off. "Look - here's me with my curlers in, chasing over England after my date!"

They all laughed, perched high up there on the tractor in the snow. And Mario gave Nell a kiss.

"Yeuch!" said Bob and Jack together.

6
Christmas

"Happy Christmas, sleepy-head!" It was Mum, kissing him awake. For the first time in his life, Bob had to be woken up on Christmas morning, he was so tired after the trek the day before. But at least they had managed to get back without any of the grown-ups noticing there was anything wrong.

"Last Christmas of the war, Bob!" Mum said.

"And last Christmas without Dad!" added Bob. They smiled at each other.

Nell was already downstairs, and they all sat down to open presents together.

As usual it was Nell that made them all laugh and forget about Dad not being there. She handed Mum a heavy round present.

"Read the label!" said Nell.

"Bottled stockings?" Mum pulled the wrapping off. Inside was a bottle of gravy browning.

"Now you can paint your legs too!"

But after they stopped laughing, Nell pulled out a smaller softer parcel and handed it to Mum.

"This is your real present," she said. "Thanks for making me part of the family." Inside was a pair of real stockings.

"Nell! However did you manage to get these?"

"Never mind that," replied Nell. "My mum can get a few things in London you can't get here – you can wear them for that first dance when your hubby gets back!"

They were all going to the farm for Christmas lunch.

"Mum," said Bob, after breakfast, "will Mario be having lunch with us all?"

"Yes, I suppose so," said Mum. "Why?"

"Could we make him one of those pizza things he was talking about, to make him feel more at home?" Mum and Nell looked at each other.

"Why not?" said Mum. "Let's have a go."

And so it was that they spent Christmas morning 1944 cooking Italian food in that small kitchen in the English countryside – or trying to, at least.

"He said bread at the bottom," said Bob. So they cut a thick slice of bread.

"And tomatoes," said Mum. "I've got some bottled tomatoes from the summer." So they spread some tomatoes on the top.

"Then cheese," said Nell. She got out her week's cheese ration – she got extra because she was in the Land Army – and cut it up into small pieces. Then they put it in the oven for a few minutes. They all stared at it doubtfully when they took it out.

"It's just cheese on toast with tomatoes," said Nell, flatly.

"Well, we did what he said," said Mum. "It's obviously what they like over there in foreign parts." And they put it in a dish and carried it carefully to the farm.

At lunchtime they were gathered round the table in the dining room, the room that was kept for special occasions. Mario was sitting next to Nell, and Bob was sitting beside Jack. Mario looked much happier today. He bent his head and whispered something to Nell and Bob saw him squeeze her hand. She smiled back at

him, and then blushed when she noticed
Bob watching.

She turned and
whispered to Bob.
"It's good news,
Bob. Someone
brought
another
letter over
from the camp
this morning –
Mario's
mother is
much
better."

Just then
Auntie May called Bob through into the
kitchen. She handed him the 'pizza' on a
serving dish.

"Here you are, lad, since it was your

idea. I'll take the turkey – you take the pizza!" And in they went together, carrying the Christmas lunch, one English, one Italian.

Mario's face was full of amazement when Bob put the pizza down in front of him.

"Is wonderful!" he said, and Bob could see tears in his eyes. "Thank you, thank you. One day you come to Italy, and I cook for you, when the war is over!"

"Here's to that!" said Uncle Leonard, and he lifted his glass. "Let's drink to when the war is over!"

And together they drank a toast to the end of the war, when everyone would finally be at home.

Britain in the Second World War

Britain and France declared war on Germany in September 1939, but by the middle of 1940 Britain was left to fight alone after France was occupied by Germany. At this time Italy joined the German side. For a long time

everyone was afraid that Germany would invade Britain too. Many British towns and cities were bombed and many people were killed.

In 1941 the Soviet Union and America joined the British side against Germany and Italy, and together they planned how to defeat the Germans. They were known as 'the Allies'.

Things looked very bad for the Allies for a long time, until they defeated the Germans and Italians in North Africa in the middle of 1943. Soon afterwards Allied troops landed in Italy and by September Italy made peace.

At last, in June 1944, on D-Day, thousands of Allied troops crossed the Channel from England to France and began to drive the German army out of France. At the same time the German army was being pushed back from Italy and Eastern Europe.

Prisoners of War

In this story, Mario is a made-up character, but there were many Italian and German prisoners in Britain during the Second World War. There were over 600 prisoner-of-war (POW) camps all over Britain, where enemy soldiers were taken after they had been captured. They were well treated in the camps, although, as for everyone else in Britain, the food was dull and not always very plentiful. Life was also dull, and prisoners played cards or made board games to pass the time. In some camps they formed orchestras and choirs, and performed plays to keep themselves busy. Many played football.

Some German and Italian prisoners of war worked on farms, because many farm workers had gone to fight in the war. After Italy surrendered to Britain and her allies, Italian prisoners had more freedom, although they were not allowed to go back to Italy until after the war. Some Italians went to live on farms where they were working. Many made friends with British people, and some fell in love with local girls.

Rationing

Soon after the war started everyone was issued with ration books. This meant they were allowed a fixed amount of certain foods depending on how many points they had. There was not as much food to go round, because many ships bringing food across the sea were sunk by German submarines. During the war many foods were rationed – bacon, ham, sugar, butter, meat, tea, margarine, cheese, cooking fat, jam, marmalade, treacle, syrup, eggs, milk and sweets. Lots of foods were hardly available at all – like bananas.

Everyone was encouraged to grow as much food as they could at home, so there were always plenty of vegetables. People living on farms, like Jack's family, could get food more easily than people living in towns.

Pick up a SPARKS to read exciting tales of what life was really like for ordinary people.

TALES OF ROWDY ROMANS
1. The Great Necklace Hunt
978 0 7496 8505 8
2. The Lost Legionary
978 0 7496 8506 5
3. The Guard Dog Geese
978 0 7496 8507 2
4. A Runaway Donkey
978 0 7496 8508 9

TALES OF A TUDOR TEARAWAY
1. A Pig called Henry
978 0 7496 8501 0
2. A Horse called Deathblow
978 0 7496 8502 7
3. Dancing for Captain Drake
978 0 7496 8503 4
4. Birthdays are a Serious Business
978 0 7496 8504 1

TRAVELS OF A YOUNG VICTORIAN
1. The Golden Key
978 0 7496 8509 6
2. Poppy's Big Push
978 0 7496 8510 2
3. Poppy's Secret
978 0 7496 8511 9
4. The Lost Treasure
978 0 7496 8512 6